ADVENTURE
#5

BOB

and the Surprisingly Slobbery Attack of the Dog-Wash Doggies

BY **L. Bob Rovetch**   ILLUSTRATED BY **Dave Whamond**

chronicle books · san francisco

For tremendously terrific Thea and indubitably incredible Isabel, who love all animals, no matter how slobbery —L. R.

Text © 2007 by Lissa Rovetch.
Illustrations © 2007 by Dave Whamond.
All rights reserved.

Series design by Mary Beth Fiorentino.
Book design by Mariana Oldenburg.
Typeset in Clarendon and Agenda.
The illustrations in this book were rendered in ink,
watercolor washes, and Prismacolor.
Manufactured in China.

Library of Congress Cataloging-in-Publication Data
Rovetch, Lissa.
Hot Dog and Bob and the surprisingly slobbery attack of the dog-
wash doggies : adventure #5 / by L. Bob Rovetch ; illustrated by Dave
Whamond.
p. cm.
Summary: When alien dogs visit Lugenheimer Elementary School during
the fifth-grade fund-raiser—a dog wash—to select human pets
for their home planet, Bowwowwowwow, Bob and Clementine
and their superhero friend, Hot Dog, must stop them.
ISBN-13: 978-0-8118-5745-1 (library edition)
ISBN-10: 0-8118-5745-X (library edition)
ISBN-13: 978-0-8118-5746-8 (pbk.)
ISBN-10: 0-8118-5746-8 (pbk.)
[1. Dogs—Fiction. 2. Kidnapping—Fiction. 3. Frankfurters—Fiction.
4. Extraterrestrial beings—Fiction. 5. Schools—Fiction. 6. Humorous
stories.] I. Whamond, Dave, ill. II. Title.
PZ7.R784Hov 2007
[Fic]—dc22
2006023586

Distributed in Canada by Raincoast Books
9050 Shaughnessy Street, Vancouver, British Columbia V6P 6E5

10 9 8 7 6 5 4 3 2 1

Chronicle Books LLC
680 Second Street, San Francisco, CA 94107

www.chroniclekids.com

Contents

Chapter 1: The Dog Wash 5

Chapter 2: Visigors! 11

Chapter 3: The Pet-Shortage Problem 17

Chapter 4: Just Little Old Me 23

Chapter 4¾: Barfalot's Revenge 27

Chapter 5: Ears Are Ears 31

Chapter 6: Barfalot Gets Bubbled 37

Chapter 7: Hot Dog's Excuse 43

Chapter 8: You're Not My Mommy! 49

Chapter 9: Angel in Disguise 57

Chapter 9½: A Robot or Something 63

Chapter 10: Sneakily Sneaky 67

Chapter 11: It Wasn't a Dream 71

Chapter 12: Dude! I *Love* This Thing! 75

Chapter 13: The Bun Attack Is Back 81

Chapter 14: Doggy-Slobber Nightmares 89

Chapter 15: The Royal Purple Potato of Bravery 93

Chapter 1

The Dog Wash

"Regular or fancy wash?" I asked Priscilla Popsicle and her puffy Pekingese puppy.

"Oh, the fancy wash, of course!" said Priscilla. "Only the best for little Pipsi here!"

"Your dog's name is Pipsi?" I asked, trying unbelievably hard not to crack up.

"Pipsi Pookypie the Fourteenth," Priscilla said proudly. "She happens to be a priceless purebred, and if you harm one little hair on her perfect little head, you'll be very, very sorry!"

"Trust me," I said, taking her money and her dog. "You have absolutely nothing to worry about."

Unfortunately, I've never been more wrong in my life. Priscilla Popsicle was about to have plenty to worry about. And I mean plenty!

In case you don't already know, my name is Bob, and I'm a fifth-grader at Lugenheimer Elementary School. A forgetful superhero hot dog got beamed into my lunch box from the planet Dogzalot a few months ago and told me I'd been picked by his leader, the Big Bun, to help defend Earth against space-alien attacks. My best friend, Clementine, who always seems to get mixed up in the mess, is the only one besides me who ever remembers anything about Hot Dog or the visitors at all.

Anyway, getting back to the story, my teacher, Miss Lamphead, decided we were going to have a dog wash instead of the usual car wash for our big class fund-raiser. It was a sunny Saturday morning, and a bunch of kids showed up to get their puppies pampered.

My good friend Marco and I were on the Greeting and Money-Collecting Committee.

We were trying to do our job, but we kept getting distracted by what was going on with Clementine. She was stuck on the Spray-and-Wash Committee with our mean and demented class bully, Barfalot, and his brothers, Pigburt and Slugburt, who (let's see, how do I put this politely?) aren't exactly the sharpest tools in the shed, if you know what I mean.

"Oh, my darlin', oh, my darlin', oh, my darlin' Clementine," Barfalot sang, "you look exactly like a doggy; dreadful sorry, Clementine!"

"Wait," said Pigburt. "That's not how the words go, is it?"

"If Barfalot says that's how the words go, then that's how they go," said Slugburt.

"Oh, my goodness," Clementine said, spraying Barfalot with the dog-washing hose. "This thing is going crazy. I can't control it. It must have a mind of its own."

"Oh, no!" said Pigburt. "The hose is going crazy! We'd better run for our lives!"

"Oh, no!" said Slugburt. "We'd better run for our lives!"

"The hose isn't going crazy!" dripped Barfalot. "The girl is! She soaked me on purpose!"

"I'm sure I haven't the foggiest idea what you're talking about!" Clementine said innocently.

"You'd better watch out, darlin' Clementine," Barfalot snarled, "'cause when nobody's lookin', I'm going to get you back—bad!"

"*Ooo!*" Clementine fake-shivered. "I'm *sooooo* scared!"

Chapter 2

Visigors!

Back at the greeting and money-collecting table, things were getting interesting.

"Hello, boy," said a bulldog wearing a uniform. "I'll take one of those extra-fancy washes."

"Sure thing, sir," said Marco. "That'll be five dollars, please."

"Um, Marco," I said, kicking him under the table. "Don't you see anything wrong with this picture?"

"What?" said Marco. "It's five bucks for an extra-fancy wash, and the dog just gave me five bucks, so—"

"So . . . ," I said, waiting for Marco to get a clue.

"So . . . dogs aren't supposed to talk and wear uniforms and pay for their own grooming needs?" Marco said, looking a little sick to his stomach.

"Bingo!" I nodded.

"I'll take an extra-fancy wash, too," said a poodle wearing a uniform, as she took a wallet out of her purse. "Oh, and how much for a nail trim? I'm way overdue for a nail trim!"

A bunch of different thoughts were racing through my head. These people-ish dogs seemed perfectly friendly. And if I hadn't known better, I probably would have thought they were totally cool. But, after several totally uncool extraterrestrial invasions, I did know better—way better!

"Um, just a minute, ma'am," I said. "If you'll just wait here, I'll go find out if we're offering nail-trimming service today."

"And a shiny-coat treatment!" the poodle added. "A dog can never be too shiny, you know!"

"Yes, ma'am," I said, "I'll find out about that, too."

"Hey! Where are you going?" whispered Marco. "You know we're not offering any of those fancy-treatment things!"

"Just keep 'em busy!" I said. "I'll be right back!"

"Um, nice w-weather we're h-having, d-don't you th-think?" I heard Marco stutter as I ran over to the spray-and-wash area.

"Clementine!" I said. "You have to come with me!"

"And leave these sweet little puppies alone with—them?" She said, pointing at the Terrible

Triplets. "That would be flat-out animal cruelty!"

"Listen to me," I said. "We have . . . V-I-S-I-G-O-R-S!"

"Visigors?" said Clementine. "What the heck are visigors?"

"Not *visigors* with a *g*!" I said. "*Visitors*! With a *t*!"

"Well, you didn't spell it with a *t*," said Clementine. "You definitely spelled it with a *g*!"

"Whatever!" I said, pulling her by the hand. "Let's just hope they're as friendly as they look."

Chapter 3

The Pet-Shortage Problem

When we got back to the greeting and money-collecting area, Marco was still talking to the dog people.

"You seem like a good little boy," said the poodle. "Are you a good little boy?"

"I don't know," said Marco. "I guess my mom thinks I'm okay."

"Oh, no, Stanley!" The poodle lady said to the bulldog man. "This one has a mother!"

"Now, Doris," said Stanley, "don't you go gettin' soft on me here. Our job is to round up the kids—not to worry about their mommies."

"Yes, I suppose you're right," said Doris. "This boy would make some owner back on Bowwow-wowwow a fine little pet!"

"So much for your friendly-visitor theory!" Clementine hissed at me.

"Look, Doris," Stanley said, pointing at Clementine. "That yellow-haired female looks like a healthy one."

"Although her nose isn't terribly attractive," said Doris. "She's obviously not show quality."

"Still," said Stanley, "I betcha plenty of owners would like a chubby little mutt like her."

"Chubby little mutt?" said Clementine. "Did he just call me a chubby little mutt?"

"Let's not rush into things, Stanley," said Doris. "Just look around this place. We have so many adorable children to choose from."

"Are these guys talking about what I think they're talking about?" Clementine whispered.

"No need to whisper, dear," said Doris. "We dogs have a highly developed sense of hearing. And if you were thinking we're talking about choosing children to bring back to our needy pet owners back home on Bowwowwowwow, then, yes—you'd be exactly right!"

"Yep," Stanley drooled, a rawhide chew stick hanging out of the corner of his mouth. "We got us a real pet shortage goin' on up there. Course no self-respecting dog wants an ugly old adult person for a pet anymore. So when our cute little people pets grow up, we put 'em out to pasture."

"And seeing as it's been several years since our last roundup," Doris added, "Bowwowwowwow is stuck with pastures full of useless old grown-up people and almost no cute little pet-worthy people at all!"

"Well, gee, . . . it sure has been great chattin' with ya," Clementine said, pulling me back toward the spray-and-wash area. "But if you'll excuse us, we've got to get back to work now—lots of dogs to wash, you know. Yes, indeedy—lots and lots of dogs to wash!"

"Oh, look at that one!" Doris said, pointing at Priscilla Popsicle as we left.

"Wait! What about Marco?" I said to Clementine. "He's our friend. We can't just leave him!"

"What about everyone?" said Clementine. "If you don't hurry up and find your flying-weenie superhero partner guy, life as we know it will be over for all of us!"

Chapter 4

Just Little Old Me

I didn't get it. Why wasn't Hot Dog showing up?
Back in the old days (a few months ago), Hot
Dog always came to Earth before the aliens.
Then, after the first couple of invasions, he
started getting more—I don't know—relaxed!

Before I had a chance to say another thing,
I heard a huge cry for help. It sounded like this:
"HELLLLLLLP!!!"

I turned to ask Clementine if she'd heard it
too, but she was gone! Splitsville! Had she run
away? This was no time to leave me on my own.
What was I supposed to do without Hot Dog

and now without Clementine, too? How could she do this to me? We were supposed to be best friends.

I was mad at my now ex–best friend for leaving me to deal with Doris and Stanley all by myself. But who could blame her really? To tell you the truth, I have no idea why I didn't just walk out with her right then and there.

So there I was. No Clementine, no Hot Dog, just little old me—and them. I took a deep breath, counted to ten, and headed back toward the greeting and money-collecting area to face my destiny.

Chapter 4¾

Barfalot's Revenge

"Oops! Watch your step!" Barfalot said, tripping me with the hose.

I didn't fall down right away. First I slipped around on the soapy blacktop, trying to catch my balance. Then I fell down. I'm pretty good with numbers, but I can't even count how many times Barfalot has tripped me since first grade.

"Ha, ha, that was awesome!" laughed Pigburt.

"Totally awesome!" laughed Slugburt.

"I couldn't get your little girlfriend back for soaking me," said Barfalot, "so I decided to get

you instead. Good one, huh?"

"She's not my girlfriend, jerk!" I sputtered.
"She's not really even my friend anymore."

Barfalot, Pigburt and Slugburt just stood
there laughing while I slipped and slid my way

back into standing position. Then I heard it again: "HELLLLLLLP!"

It was definitely Marco's voice. I ran back as fast as I could.

Chapter 5

Ears Are Ears

Stanley and Doris had definitely been busy.
A barbed-wire fence now surrounded the field
next to the dog wash. The kids were on the
inside, and the dogs were running around
on the outside.

"Don't worry, Pipsi Pookypie the Fourteenth!"
I heard Priscilla Popsicle calling to her Pekingese,
"I won't let those terrible monsters take you away!"

Poor Priscilla obviously didn't get the deal.
Stanley and Doris weren't going to take little
Pipsi away. They were going to take little

Priscilla away! I was so busy staring at all the action on the field I almost didn't notice who was walking straight toward me!

"This roundup's goin' faster than we expected," snorted Stanley.

"Yes, we make quite a team," Doris said, fluttering her eyelashes at Stanley.

I ducked behind the towel rack. My heart was pounding like a jackhammer. When I finally worked up the courage to peek through a crack in the towels, I saw the two of them sitting in the drying and grooming area.

Stanley's hat and drool-covered rawhide stick were resting on the table, and he was smoothing his head with one of our special Lugenheimer Elementary Dog-

Wash Fund-Raiser brushes. Doris was busy fixing her hairstyle, too.

"Stanley," she said, "do you think my ears look better in or out of my cap?"

"Ears are ears," Stanley said, scratching an itch. "We'd better go take care of business and call for the transporter."

"Oh, Stanley," said Doris, "speaking of business, there's something I've been wanting to ask you."

"What's that?" Stanley asked, popping the slimy stick back into his mouth.

"Well, I've been thinking," said Doris. "We have room for only a few children in the transporter, and this planet has so very many boys and girls. If we were to set up a permanent training and transporting base right here and now, we'd never run out. We'd have a constant supply—more than enough pets for every single owner on Bowwowwowwow! Just think of the

great service we'd be providing! And you and I would have lots and lots of time together—you know—getting to know each other better. What do you say, Stanley?"

"Why not?" he drooled. "Once we load this batch onto the transporter, we'll set up shop here—permanently."

Chapter 6

Barfalot Gets Bubbled

This plan to make my school's playing field into a permanent people-pet training and transport base didn't sound good. But I wasn't sure how terrified to be. True, Doris and Stanley had put up a barbed-wire fence. But that was it. Come to think of it, I couldn't remember seeing either of them do a single magic thing.

"Hey, Slip 'n' Slide," yelled Barfalot, "you can run, but you can't hide! We see you behind those towels!"

"Yeah, we see you!" said Pigburt.

"Yeah, we see you!" said Slugburt.

The Terrible Triplets! I wasn't so all alone after all.

"I'm not hiding from you pea brains!" I whispered. "I'm hiding from them!"

"Oh, look over there, Stanley!" said Doris. "We missed those three little boy children!"

"Oh, yeah," drooled Stanley. "Not exactly what you'd call cute little suckers, are they?"

"Well, I can't say I recognize the breed," said Doris. "But we might as well toss them in with the others. After all, there are some dogs who actually prefer to adopt really strange-looking pets."

Stanley took the slobbery chew stick out of his mouth, pointed it at Barfalot, Pigburt and Slugburt and mumbled, "*Bow-ruffy-wow-ruffy woof-woof-woof!*"

A bright light shot out of the stick, zipped around the Terrible Triplets and surrounded them in a glowing green dog-bone-shaped bubble. Then Stanley used the slobbery stick as some kind of remote-control device and guided the bubble over to the playing field.

"Beautifully done!" Doris cheered as she clapped her fuzzy poodle paws together.

"Aw, that was nothin'," blushed Stanley. "Just wait till we get onto that field. Then we're really going to have some fun!"

So much for thinking they might be harmless. As Doris and Stanley left to have fun on the field, I got down on my knees and pleaded.

"I know you probably can't hear me, Hot Dog," I whispered desperately, "but I really can't handle this mission without you. So if you could possibly find it in your hot-doggy heart to stop by just for a little bit, well, uh, I could really, really use a hand here!"

Chapter 7

Hot Dog's Excuse

No answer. I didn't know if Hot Dog couldn't hear me, or if he'd just up and decided to quit being a superhero like Clementine just up and decided to quit being my friend.

When I got up and looked over at the field, I could hardly believe my eyes. Stanley had made an entire obstacle course out of glowing beams of light, and Doris was making all the kids do tricks!

"Looks like quite a show," said a familiar-sounding little voice.

I looked over to see Hot Dog sitting on the edge of a chair.

"Okay, mister!" I said. "You seriously took too long to show up this time! You'd better have a good excuse! No, you know what? Scratch that! Never mind! Don't bother! Forget it! I don't even want to hear your useless excuse! If Clementine can leave, then so can I! I am officially resigning from the position of your Earth partner, which, by the way, I never chose in the first dumb place!"

"Whoa! Slow down there, Bobby Boy!" said Hot Dog. "I can't blame ya for blowin' your top. You've got yourself every right in the world to be hoppin' mad! But listen, kid—you shoulda seen me tacklin' that two-headed fire-breathing tiger-dragon up there on Castlelandia! Just when

I finally had that sucker beat, his three-headed lava-breathing pretty-boy daddy decided to show up! I'm tellin' ya, I was lucky to make it off of that planet in one piece! You understand, don't ya partner?"

Right in the middle of my absolutely not
understanding, kids started floating up above
the field in glowing green dog-bone bubbles
just like the one the Terrible Triplets were in.

"Come on, kiddo," Hot Dog smiled. "Looks
like we've got us a job to do!"

He straightened out his cape, put his arms
up Superman-style, and flew toward the field.

Don't ask me why I went running after him.
I just did.

"Hey, Hot Dog," I yelled as I ran, "shouldn't
we have some kind of a plan here?"

"Sorry, kid!" he yelled back. "No time for
a plan! We're going to have to play this baby
by ear!"

Chapter 8

You're Not My Mommy!

When we got to the field, Hot Dog swooped down, grabbed me by the back of my collar and used some kind of super-weenie strength to lift me up and over the barbed-wire fence.

"Well, well, what have we here?" asked Doris.

"Looks like a delicious flyin' snack," Stanley drooled over Hot Dog.

"I'm no snack, Jack!" my partner exclaimed. "Hot Dog's my name. And fightin' bad stuff's my game!"

"You're barkin' up the wrong tree there, little snack guy," said Stanley. "We're not bad stuff!"

"Not at all," said Doris. "In fact, we're here for a very good cause!"

"Oh, yeah?" I said. "If you think trapping and stealing kids is a good cause, then you'd better think again!"

"Oh, look," said Doris. "It's that funny little boy who went to find out about the nail-trimming and shiny-coat treatments."

"Nobody will want to adopt a troublemaker with an attitude like that," said Stanley. "We might as well get rid of him right here and now."

He took the slobbery stick out of his mouth, aimed it at me, and mumbled, "*Bow-ruffy-wow-ruffy-woof-woof-woof!*"

This time it was a bright red beam of light that shot out of the icky stick. But I barely had the chance to freak out about dying before Doris threw herself in front of me. I still don't know exactly what happened, but the light just bounced right off her poodley body, and I was totally fine!

"I've been looking everywhere for a fearless guard boy like this one!" Doris said, patting me on the head. "From now on, little pet, you're mine! All mine!"

"I don't think so!" Hot Dog said, making a move to press one of his handy-dandy bun buttons and fix everything.

But unfortunately for us, Stanley beat him to the punch. "*Bow-ruffy-wow-ruffy-woof-woof-woof!*" the bulldog said as he zapped.

The next thing Hot Dog and I knew, we were wearing matching orange light-beam harnesses, and Doris was holding our leashes!

"What am I supposed to do with this thing?" she said, looking down her nose at Hot Dog.

"Just tie 'em both up for now," Stanley said, licking his lips. "I'm savin' the snack for later."

Doris tied the ends of our leashes to the barbed-wire fence, and Stanley secured them with an impenetrable light-beam barrier.

"You be a good widdle boy," Doris said, patting me on the head. "Mommy will be back for her cutie wootie just as soon as she finishes her worky worky. Okeydokey?"

"You're not my mommy!" I snapped.

"A little visit to training school and he won't remember he ever even had a mother!" Doris cackled to Stanley as they walked away.

"Did you hear that?" I panicked. "She's going to brainwash me!"

"Never mind that," said Hot Dog. "He's going to eat me!"

We were both trying our hardest to rip off our harnesses, but it was no use.

"I don't know what kind of crazy light beam these things are made out of," said Hot Dog, "but it appears to have deactivated my bun but-

tons. I hate to say this, partner, but unless an angel decides to show up . . ."

Hot Dog collapsed on the ground, put his face in his hot-doggy little hands and sighed. He never finished his sentence; he didn't have to. We both knew perfectly well that unless a miracle happened, our planet would become one big people-pet school, I would become Doris the poodle's brainwashed guard boy, and Hot Dog would become Stanley the slobbery bulldog's very next snack!

Chapter 9

Angel in Disguise

"Did somebody call for an angel?" asked a voice.

Hot Dog and I turned around to see Clementine wearing the worst dog costume you've ever seen. I don't know what got into us, but we both just started laughing uncontrollably.

"What do you think you're laughing at?" yelled Clementine. "If anyone should be laughing, it's me! I've been watching this whole disaster from across the street, on old Mr. Burpmeister's roof. And it doesn't take a genius to know you don't just go charging into enemy territory without having some type of disguise on!"

Even though I was laughing at Clementine,
I was totally relieved to see her. And even
though her dog disguise was beyond pitiful,
I had to admit she was actually kind of right.
Hot Dog and I had been idiots for barging onto
that field without a plan.

"You came back!" I said. "I thought you'd left
for good!"

"I'm not that bad a friend," said Clementine.
"I just needed some time to think and
make a plan."

"Oh, that's cool," I said, trying to
act like it was no big deal. "But
how did you get over the fence?"

"I didn't get over it," she said, taking a shovel out from under her dog disguise. "I got under it!"

"Miss Clementine," Hot Dog said all seriously, "you risked your life to come back here and save us. If we ever make it out of this mess alive, I promise to see to it that you are awarded Dogzalot's highest medal of honor, the Royal Purple Potato of Bravery."

"The Royal Purple what of what?" asked Clementine.

"It's our version of your country's distinguished honor, the Purple Heart," Hot Dog explained. "It's not every day that—"

"The power's in the chew stick!" I interrupted frantically. "The chew stick shoots out the light beams!"

"He's right," said Hot Dog. "You gotta get that stick so we can reverse the light beams, break out of these harnesses and start savin' the world!"

"Ohhh-kaaay," said Clementine. "And I'm supposed to do that exactly how?"

"Just be sneaky," yawned Hot Dog. "Just be very, very sneakily sneaky!"

"Um, could you be a little more specific?" said Clementine. "I mean, there's kind of a lot at

stake here, including a little thing I like to
call . . . my life!"

But Hot Dog couldn't be any more specific
about that or anything else. He'd fallen asleep,
and we couldn't wake him back up!

A Robot or Something

"Hot Dog! You have to wake up!" I said, shaking him kind of hard.

"Wake him, don't break him!" said Clementine.

"If the light beam deactivated his bun buttons," I panicked, "maybe it deactivated other stuff, too!"

"Hot Dog's not a machine," said Clementine. "He's a living, breathing flesh-and-blood being. You can't just deactivate someone unless he's like . . . a robot or something."

The second Clementine said the word *robot* we both just stopped and stared at each other.

"No way!" I said. "He would have told us if he were a robot."

"Do we really know that for sure?" asked Clementine. "Think about it, Bob. Do we really know anything about Hot Dog for sure?"

"We know he comes from Dogzalot, where everyone's a superhero hot dog," I said. "We know he believes in peace, respects the Big Bun and—"

"And what?!" said Clementine. "Face it, we basically know nothing about the guy. Take his parents, for example. Have you ever heard him say one word about his parents? Maybe he has no parents. Maybe he was never even born at all. Maybe he was manufactured in some factory!"

I was all mixed up. I couldn't think straight. Could Clementine be right? Could the feisty little weenie in charge of saving our whole big planet be nothing more than a machine? I couldn't stop to think about it. Robot or not, we had to get that stick and wake up Hot Dog!

Chapter 10

Sneakily Sneaky

Clementine bravely grabbed some branches off the ground and traded her lousy dog disguise in for a lousy tree disguise. I watched helplessly as she sneakily sneaked her way across the field, sneakily sneaked the chew stick out of Stanley's back pocket, then sneakily sneaked her way back over to Hot Dog and me.

"I can't believe you actually got it!" I said. "Quick! Aim it at Hot Dog before it's too late!"

"Earth to Bob," said Clementine. "We can't just aim and shoot! Who knows what could happen! Besides, we need to reverse the light beams, not make more of them!"

Hot Dog's snoring was changing from loud and snorty to quiet and gaspy. We had to figure out how the stick worked—immediately!

"Jackpot!" said Clementine. "Look! Underneath the slobber there's a capital *R* on this end! That has to stand for *reverse!*"

I pointed the stick with the *R* end facing Hot Dog and said, "Please, oh, please, oh, *pleeeeease* reverse!" But nothing happened.

"Maybe pointing isn't enough," said Clementine. "The bulldog must have done something else. Come on, Bob, you have to think!"

"I don't know," I said. "He might have said something—*bark, woof*—you know, something like that."

"Think, Bob!" Clementine begged. "The fate of all Earth's children is in your hands!"

Chapter 11

It Wasn't a Dream

I couldn't take the pressure.

"I can't do it," I said, sweating like a pig in a fur coat in a sauna. "I'm never going to remember the right words!"

"Yes, you are!" said Clementine. "The whole reason the Big Bun picked you to be Hot Dog's Earth partner in the first place was your excellent memory! Come on, just try one more time!"

Right when I was ready to give up for good, Hot Dog let out a sad, squeaky little gurgle.

"*Bow-ruffy-wow-ruffy-woof-woof-woof!*" I said without even thinking.

Luckily, it worked like a charm! Hot Dog's light-beam harness got sucked right into the chew stick! It shot back so hard and fast the sheer force of it knocked me flat on my butt!

SLOORP

"You'll never believe the dream I had,"

Hot Dog yawned. "There were these two

dogs in uniforms and—"

"It wasn't a dream!" Clementine said. "Don't

you remember? Before you went to sleep? Dogs

taking over the world? People pets? All that fun

stuff?"

While Hot Dog tried to wake up and remember,

Clementine and I tried not to get stampeded by

Stanley and Doris, who just so happened to be

running our way.

Chapter 12

Dude! I *Love* This Thing!

"There it is!" barked Stanley. "They have it!"

"I don't understand," Doris said, screeching to a halt. "What would my perfect widdle pet guard boy be doing with our light activator?"

"I'm not your pet, lady—er, I mean *doggy*!" I said, pointing the stick at myself. "*Bow-ruffy-wow-ruffy-woof-woof-woof!*"

It worked again! This time my harness got vacuumed up!

"Why don't you be a good little boy and hand that thing over before somebody gets hurt?" slobbered Stanley. "Then I can eat my tasty snack here, and we can all just get right on back to business as usual."

But being in control of that powerful device made me feel like I could do anything!

"I believe my partner already told you he is not a snack!" I said. "And for your information, business as usual at Lugenheimer Elementary does not happen to include you two kidnapper weirdos!"

I pointed the nonreverse end of the stick at Stanley and Doris, said, "*Bow-ruffy-wow-ruffy-woof-woof-woof*," and—BAM—they were trapped in a glowing cage of bright blue light!

"Dude!" I said, "I *love* this thing!"

Hot Dog jumped up, grabbed the magical stick out of my hand and flew away, saying, "Gotta hurry up before—"

"Before what?" I called after him.

"I think what the snack was trying to say," Doris said, pointing up above our heads, "is before our transporter comes to load up our first pet shipment to bring back to Bowwowwowwow. But too bad for you we signaled our transporter hours ago, so . . . Oh, well—*c'est la vie!*"

"Say la what?" asked Clementine.

"*C'est la vie,*" said Doris. "It's French for 'that's life.'"

"I didn't know you spoke French," Stanley said all excitedly.

"There's a lot you don't know about me," Doris said, fixing her ears.

Clementine and I looked up to see the transporter hovering above the field. It was a spaceship shaped like a bone. A blinding tunnel of light was pouring out of it and sucking up the glowing green bubble prisons right before our eyes!

Chapter 13

The Bun Attack Is Back

Hot Dog was flying circles around the transporter. He tried the chew stick in reverse mode to suck up the tunnel of light. When that failed, he used the other end to shoot zillions of light beams directly at the transporter itself. But nothing worked. The last green bubble disappeared into the light. The door closed, and the transporter started to hover away.

"Oh, no!" cried Clementine.

"Don't get too much exercise up there," Stanley yelled at Hot Dog. "I like my snacks with plenty of fat on 'em!"

"Forget this rawhide reject!" Hot Dog said,

flinging the stick away. "Ladies

and gentlemen, the bun

attack is back!"

He pushed one secret

bun button, and gallons

of ketchup squirted out

all over the transporter. He

pushed another, and tons of relish

coated the thing. A third bun button released

pounds of chopped onions. And even though the transporter was already spiraling down, Hot Dog pushed the mustard and sauerkraut buttons. SPLAT!!! SPLAT!!!

The good news was Hot Dog's bun attack grounded the transporter. The bad news was the thing was so covered in a gigantic mountain of slime that I couldn't imagine ever seeing Marco, Priscilla or any of our other poor trapped friends again!

"I'm warnin' you," Stanley drooled. "If you don't let us out of here on the double, you're in real big trouble!"

"Oh, yeah?" said Clementine. "Well, we're out here, and you're in there. From where I'm standing, it looks like you two are the ones who are in trouble!"

"Good heavens!" complained Doris. "Why won't they understand? Dogs don't belong on leashes—people do!"

"How's about we play us a little game?" said Hot Dog. "A little game called Let's Make a Deal!"

"What do you have in mind, Snack Man?" slobbered Stanley.

"Well," said Hot Dog, "for starters you can call me by my real name: Robot Number Three Thousand Seven Hundred and Sixty-Four."

Clementine and I looked at each other in complete and utter horror. It shouldn't have mattered to us if he was flesh and blood or not. But it did. It really did!

"Ha! Just pullin' yer leg'!" Hot Dog laughed.

"I heard you two talkin' in my sleep. For your information, I happen to have two perfectly nice parents, thank you very much! As a matter of fact, I promised to pay my dear old mother a visit after work today, so if you don't mind, I'd like to wrap this mission up and get a move on!"

"All right!" barked Stanley. "You've got our light activator; we've got nothin' but a big blue cage. What kind of a deal we talkin' about here?"

"We agree to let you out," said Hot Dog, "and you agree to go home and never set foot or tail on this planet again! Is it a deal?"

"Hold on a second," slobbered Stanley. "Let me check with my fiancée, here. What do you think, Dory, baby? Should we make the deal?"

"Oh, Stanley!" cried Doris. "Are you proposing marriage to me? Oh, Stanley! This is the most wonderful day of my entire life!"

"Wow!" said Clementine. "I definitely didn't see that one coming."

Chapter 14

Doggy-Slobber Nightmares

After Doris accepted Stanley's proposal, that's all either of them could talk about—you know, who was coming to the wedding, where the honeymoon would be. Believe it or not, they were so excited about their big news they could hardly wait to get home.

Hot Dog pushed his famous clean-everything-up-and-return-everything-to-normal bun button, and the ketchup, relish, onions, sauerkraut and mustard were completely gone. So were Doris and Stanley and any sign at all of light beams, barbed-wire fences or people-pet training things of any kind.

"The—time—has—come—" Hot Dog said in a really weird slow voice, "for—this—ro—bot—to—go." Then he switched back to his normal voice, "I'm just pullin' yer leg again!" He laughed. "Hey, we sure do have some crazy fun together, don't we?"

"Oh, yeah," Clementine said, rolling her eyes. "Some real crazy fun!"

Hot Dog thanked us for our help, hugged us good-bye and pushed his forgetting button. A jet stream of forgetting dust sparkled behind him as he flew away.

Clementine and I knew the routine. Like always, the forgetting dust worked on everyone but us. The kids and the dogs were back at the dog wash—as if nothing out of the ordinary had ever even happened. And we got to have doggy-slobber nightmares for weeks to come.

Chapter 15

The Royal Purple Potato of Bravery

The next day Clementine came to school with something new in her backpack.

"Hey, Bob," she said, "you'll never guess what I found under my pillow this morning."

"No way!" I said. "He kept his promise?"

"Not to brag or anything," she said, admiring the potato, "but I really do deserve this. Oh, here. He left a little something for you, too."

THE END

(for now)

Visit Hot Dog and Bob's Surprisingly Slobbery Web Site for more information and fun activities:
www.chroniclebooks.com/hotdogandbob/
www.hotdogandbob.com

As an award-winning investigative reporter specializing in extraterrestrial activity, **L. Bob Rovetch** has spent hundreds of hours interviewing Bob and helping him record his amazing but true adventures. Ms. Rovetch lives across the Golden Gate Bridge from San Francisco with two perfect children and plenty of pets.

Dave Whamond wanted to be a cartoonist ever since he could pick up a crayon. During math classes he would doodle in the margin of his papers. One math teacher warned him, "You'd better spend more time on your math and less time cartooning. You can't make a living drawing funny pictures." Today Dave has a syndicated daily comic strip, called *Reality Check.* Dave has one wife, two kids, one dog, and one kidney. They all live together in Calgary, Alberta.

To host an event with the author of this book, please contact publicity@chroniclebooks.com.

Look Out!
The Foot Fighters Are Heading Your Way!

Just when you thought the world was safe! Arriving in Spring 2008 is an all-new Hot Dog and Bob adventure.

Hot Dog and Bob and the Ferociously Freaky Attack of the Foot Fighters

Game time becomes anything but ordinary when alien foot fighters challenge the Lugenheimer Elementary kids to an intergalactic soccer match! Now Hot Dog, Bob and Clementine have to defeat the yet-undefeated Foot Fighters and save Earth from being shrunken down and made into a trophy! Will Bob and Clementine ever be able to look at feet in the same way again? Find out when the adventures of Hot Dog and Bob continue.